A Christmas Carol

Keith West

EVANS BROTHERS LIMITED

Characters

Scrooge a mean old man who owns a business
Bob Cratchit a poor man who works for Scrooge
Mrs Cratchit Bob's wife
Peter Cratchit Bob's oldest son
Belinda Cratchit a younger daughter of Bob
Martha Cratchit Bob's eldest daughter
Tiny Tim Bob's crippled son
Marley's ghost ghost of Scrooge's dead partner
Ghost of Christmas Past
Ghost of Christmas Present
Ghost of Christmas Future
Nephew Fred, Scrooge's nephew
Niece Fred's wife
Clergyman
Clerk
Undertaker
Gentleman 1} charity collectors
Gentleman 2}
Young Scrooge appears as a young boy without speaking,
then as a young man
Mr Fezziwig employed the young Scrooge
Dick Wilkins non-speaking part
Fan Scrooge's sister
Bella once engaged to Scrooge
Old Bella
Bella's daughter
Husband Bella's husband
Fat Merchant
Thin Merchant
Dark-haired Merchant
Red-faced Merchant
Woman
Mrs Dilber
Boy
Man
Servant

Staging the Play

If you intend to perform the play, you should not need many sets or backdrops.

Using a traditional school stage, the first part of the action (burial of Marley) can take place at the front of the stage. Scrooge's office can be to one side of the stage. It will need to remain there throughout the play. All you need for this scene are two small desks, one for Scrooge and the other for Bob Cratchit. You could use a backdrop of wallpaper and a small fire.

Scene Two is also quite simple. The doorknob can be imaginary and Scrooge's room can be fairly bare. The only props needed are two armchairs. A backdrop of a warm fire (to contrast with the one in Scrooge's office) is all that is needed.

Scene Three opens with the same stage set as Scene Two. The school can be centre stage, you will need some chairs and desks for this scene. Scrooge's office can double up as Fezziwig's office, with just a few modifications. The rest of the action can take place at the front of the stage. If you have modern technology, why not use a whiteboard to show Scrooge and the ghost flying through the air? If not, just blacken the stage and play ghostly music as Scrooge and the Christmas Ghost travel.

Scene Four begins in Scrooge's room. The room is the same as the previous scenes, except it is decorated with Christmas things. The ghost can be seated centre stage, surrounded by Christmas foods. Bob Cratchit's dining room can be kept simple, all you really need is a long table, chairs and a Christmas cloth. The nephew and niece can act out their scenes at the front of the stage, which would minimise props and backdrops.

Scene Five. This begins with the merchants and the women and could all be acted at the front of the stage. All you will need for this scene will be Bob Cratchit's dining room, the table bare. When Scrooge sees his office, this could be quite effectively done in mime.

Scene Six can be acted out in Scrooge's office and at the stage front.

Good luck!

A Christmas Carol
Act One Scene One

Scrooge, Clergyman, Clerk and Undertaker are at the graveyard

Clergyman: *(Signing register of burial)* Well, there you have it Mr Scrooge. Your old partner in business is dead and buried.

Clerk: *(Signs register of burial)* As dead as a doornail!

Undertaker: Unless, like the ghost of Hamlet's father, he walks the battlements at night. *(Chuckles, but the other three at the graveside stare at him. Embarrassed, he coughs)*

Clerk: *(To undertaker)* Go on then!

(Undertaker signs document)

Scrooge: Huh! Over and done with, eh? *(Signs document and walks away)*

Undertaker: *(To Clergyman and Clerk, gesturing to the grave)* There lies the meanest man in the whole of London.

Clerk: Except for his partner, *(Points at departing figure of Scrooge)* old Scrooge.

Clergyman: You know why old Scrooge was in such a hurry, don't you?

(*The other two shake their heads*)

He's not so dreadfully cut up by the death of his only friend that he couldn't conduct business as usual – and get a bargain, no doubt!

(*The three men laugh, then exit. Bob Cratchit enters and sits at his desk. Scrooge stands at side of stage*)

Scrooge: (*Narrating*) Seven years fled by and I'd mostly forgotten about old Marley. I was sitting in my office one Christmas Eve. It was very cold. However, I did not allow anything other than a small fire. My clerk, Bob Cratchit, was trying to keep warm and work. My nephew entered and talked to Bob. I could hear all they were talking about.

(*Nephew enters*)

Bob: Nobody ever gives *him* the time of day. Nobody will ever say, 'My dear Scrooge, how are you? When will you come and see me?' (*Confidentially*) They daren't! No beggars ask for money, no children ask him the time. No man or woman will ever ask him the way to anywhere. (*Whispers*) They darn't. Even blind men's dogs avoid him. But what does Scrooge care? Not a jot!

Nephew: Ah, well… I'll talk to him. (*Goes over to Scrooge*) A merry Christmas, Uncle! God save you!

Scrooge: Bah, humbug!

Nephew: *(Mocking)* Christmas a humbug, Uncle? You don't mean that, I'm sure!

Scrooge: *(Annoyed)* I do! Merry Christmas? What right have you to be merry? What reason have you to be merry? You're poor enough!

Nephew: *(Laughs)* Come then, what right have you to be dismal? What reason have you to be sad? You're rich enough!

Scrooge: *(Turns back to the work on his desk)* Bah! *(Glares at nephew)* Humbug!

Nephew: *(Still cheerful)* Don't be cross, Uncle.

Scrooge: *(Annoyed)* What else can I be, when I live in such a world of fools as this? Merry Christmas? Out upon Merry Christmas! What's Christmas time to you but a time for paying bills without money; a time for finding yourself a year older, but not an hour richer? If I could work my will, every idiot who goes about with 'Merry Christmas' on his lips should be boiled with his own pudding, and buried with a stake of holly through his heart. He should!

Nephew: *(Pleading)* Uncle!

Scrooge: *(Firm)* Nephew! *(Glares at nephew)* Keep Christmas in your own way, and let me keep it in mine!

Nephew: Keep it? But you don't keep it!

Scrooge: Let me leave it alone then! Much good it has ever done you!

Nephew: *(Exasperated)* Uncle, there are many things from which I might have gained good but not gained a profit, – Christmas being one! But I have always thought of Christmas as a good time; a kind, forgiving, charitable, pleasant time of the year. In fact, the only time of year when people think of others, not so well off as themselves, as fellow passengers to the grave… and not as another race of people bound on other journeys. So, Uncle, although Christmas has never put a scrap of silver or gold in my pocket, I believe it *has* done me good and *will* do me good. I say God bless Christmas!

Bob: *(Claps)* Ha, yes, well spoken, Fred! (*Realises what he has just done, becomes embarrassed and pokes at the small fire*)

Scrooge: (*Turns angrily to Bob*) Let me hear another sound from *you* and you'll keep your Christmas by losing your job! (*Turns and glares at his nephew*) You're quite a powerful speaker, sir! I wonder you don't enter parliament.

Nephew: (*Laughs*) Don't be grumpy, Uncle. Come on, it's Christmas! Have dinner with my wife and I tomorrow.

Scrooge: Yes, yes. I'll come and see you – but I'll see you in Hell first!

Nephew: (*Shrugs shoulders*) But why? Why act like this, Uncle?

Scrooge: Why? Why did *you* get married?

Nephew: (*Surprised*) Why? Well, because I fell in love!

Scrooge: (*Almost growling*) Because you fell in love? How ridiculous! Good afternoon, goodbye!

Nephew: (*Hesitating*) But Uncle, you never came to see me *before* I was married. Why not give it a reason to see me now? I want nothing from you; I ask nothing of you. But you *are* my uncle. Why can't we just be friends?

Scrooge: Good afternoon! (*Turns to his accounts*)

Nephew: (*Upset*) I am sorry, with all my heart, to find you so determined not to enjoy Christmas, Uncle. We have never had any quarrel, so why do you act like this? But (*Becoming cheerful*) I'll keep Christmas as it should be kept. So, Merry Christmas, Uncle!

Scrooge: Bah!

Nephew: And a Happy New Year!

Scrooge: Humbug!

(Nephew goes to talk to Bob, while Bob works)

Scrooge: *(To himself)* There's another fellow, my clerk, who earns fifteen shillings a week… and a wife and family to keep… talking about a merry Christmas! I'll retire to the madhouse!

(As Scrooge's nephew leaves the office, two smartly dressed gentlemen enter. They both doff their hats when they see Scrooge)

Gentleman 1: Do I have the pleasure of addressing Mr Scrooge or Mr Marley?

Scrooge: Mr Marley died seven years ago this very day.

Gentleman 2: We have no doubt his generosity is well represented by his surviving partner.

Scrooge: *(Scowls when he hears the word 'generosity')* Not so, not so!

Gentleman 1: *(Not put off)* At this time of year, it is usual for businesses to make some *small* provision for the poor and the homeless. They suffer this time of year, sir. The cold, you know!

Scrooge: *(Annoyed)* Are there no prisons, no workhouses?

Gentleman 1: *(Surprised)* Indeed there are – but they are harsh places. We would like to raise a fund to buy the poor some meat and drink.

Gentleman 2: After all sir, it is Christmas!

Gentleman 1: *(Opens book)* How much shall we put you down for?

(Scrooge looks blankly at the gentlemen)

Gentleman 2: (*Thinking Scrooge has not understood*) We mean, how much money will you give for the poor and needy?

Scrooge: *(Very angry)* Nothing! I don't make merry at Christmas, and I can't afford to make other people happy! I support prisons and workhouses, let them go there!

Gentleman 1: Many can't go there; and many would rather die.

Scrooge: *(Shouting)* If they'd rather die, they'd better do it… and then they won't be a burden on society. Now – be off with you both!

(The gentlemen hastily leave Scrooge's office)

Helping other people! Bah! Humbug!

(A thick fog has spread over London. In the distance, Christmas carols are sung. Scrooge turns angrily to Bob)

You'll want all day off tomorrow, I suppose!

Bob: (*Timid*) If it is convenient, sir!

Scrooge: (*Angry*) It's *not* convenient and it's not fair. If I was to stop some of your wages, you'd think me mean, wouldn't you?

(*Not knowing how to react, Bob smiles faintly*)

And yet, you won't think me put upon when I pay you a day's wages for no work!

Bob: (*Weakly*) But it's only once a year!

Scrooge: (*Throwing water on the dead fire*) A poor excuse for picking my pocket every twenty-fifth of December. (*Puts on his outside coat*) But I suppose you must have the whole day! (*Buttons his coat*) Be here all the earlier the next morning!

Bob: (*Excited*) Yes, Mr Scrooge. Thank you, Mr Scrooge. (*Quietly, to himself*) You're *so* generous, Mr Scrooge.

Scrooge: Huh, well, off you go and I'll take dinner in my usual place, despite the fog and the cold.

(*Both exit*)

Scene Two

Scrooge is sitting in his room at home

Scrooge: (*Narrating*) That Christmas Eve I had just left the tavern, having enjoyed a good meal. I was content as I walked through the fog-ridden streets. I soon reached my own home. It was a large old house I'd shared with Marley. Since Marley's death, I'd rented out some of the rooms, to make even more money. On reaching home, I was about to put my hand on the door knocker when I imagined, or maybe saw, Marley's face. It appeared to me that the door knocker had become Marley's face!

Scrooge: (*Not frightened and in his room*) Pooh, pooh! I've eaten too much! Seeing Marley's face – humbug!

(*Suddenly, a bell begins to swing and chime in Scrooge's room. Then all the bells in the old house begin to chime. As the bells stop, Scrooge can hear a noise – like the dragging of heavy chains*)

Don't *ghosts* drag heavy chains?

(*The house is suddenly filled with strange noises – loud noises coming towards Scrooge's room*)

It's humbug still! I won't believe it!

(Quite suddenly, the door is flung open and a figure dragging a heavy chain walks into Scrooge's room)

I know him, it's Marley – Marley's ghost!

(Marley is dressed in his old waistcoat, trousers and boots. He is, however, all white. His chains are also white. The chains he drags hold keys, cashboxes, padlocks, ledgers, deeds and heavy purses made of steel)

How now, what do you want of me?

Marley's ghost: *(Speaking slowly and in a ghostly voice)* Much!

Scrooge: Who are you?

Marley's ghost: Ask me who I *was*.

Scrooge: *(Not afraid)* Who *were* you then? You're particular for a shade.

Marley's ghost: *(Mournful)* In life I was your partner, Jacob Marley.

Scrooge: Can you sit down?

Marley's ghost: I can.

Scrooge: (*Brisk*) Do it then.

Marley's ghost: (*Sits down in his old seat*) You don't believe in ghosts?

Scrooge: (*Hard*) No, I don't.

Marley's ghost: (*Puzzled*) Why don't you trust your senses?

Scrooge: Because little things affect them. I've just had a meal and that might affect my senses. You are… humbug! You might as well go away, you don't frighten me!

Marley's ghost: (*Shakes his chains in a frightening manner and moans loudly*) Ahhhhhhhhhhh!

Scrooge: (*Now very frightened. He falls on his knees and clasps his hands in front of his face*) Mercy! Dreadful ghost, why do you trouble me?

Marley's ghost: Man of the world, do you believe in me or not?

Scrooge: (*Still frightened*) I do, I must! But why do you spirits walk the Earth and why do they come to me?

Marley's ghost: (*Serious*) It is expected of every man that the spirit within him should walk amongst his fellow men. If that does not happen during life, the spirit must do so after death. I am doomed to wander through the world – oh, woe is me! I could have shared on this Earth and made people happy – now all I can do is warn you!

Scrooge: You are in chains, why?

Marley's ghost: I wear the chains I forged in life. I made these chains link by link and of my own free will – as *you* are doing. Your chains were as heavy as mine seven Christmas Eves ago. You have worked on them since. Your chains must be *really heavy* by now.

Scrooge: *(Shakes with fear)* My old partner, Jacob Marley, speak some comfort to me.

Marley's ghost: *(Shakes his head, which makes his chains rattle)* I have no comfort to give you, Ebenezer Scrooge. Kinder men can offer you comfort. I'm not allowed to stay, I cannot rest. I must go now.

Scrooge: *(Pleading)* Oh, offer me something of comfort, Jacob.

Marley's ghost: I came tonight to warn you. You do have a chance of escaping my fate, Ebenezer.

Scrooge: *(Relieved)* Oh, you always were a good friend to me, Jacob.

Marley's ghost: You will be haunted by three spirits.

Scrooge: (*Shaken*) I – I think – I'd rather not!

Marley's ghost: (*Serious*) Without meeting these three spirits, you cannot hope to escape my fate. Expect the first tomorrow, when the clock strikes one.

Scrooge: (*Begging Marley's ghost*) Can't I take 'em all at once and have it over and done with, Jacob?

Marley's ghost: (*Solemn*) Expect the second on the next night at the same time. The third on the next night, when the last stroke of twelve has ceased to be heard. You will never see me again. For your sake, I hope you will remember what has just passed between us!

Scrooge: How can I forget? It's not every night I see a ghost!

(*As Marley's ghost slowly leaves the room, dragging his chains, Scrooge hears noises in the air – sounds of sadness and regret. There are wailings of sorrow. Some spirits are wailing, 'Too late, too late'*)

Scene Three

Scrooge is in his room, he has fallen asleep on his chair. He is fully dressed. He awakes to the sound of twelve chimes

Scrooge: *(To himself)* Twelve? Why, it isn't possible! I can't have slept through a whole day and far into another night. Perhaps something has happened to the sun and it's twelve noon. *(He rises from his chair)* Did I see Marley's ghost or not? *(The clock strikes a quarter past twelve)* Did I see my old partner? *(The clock strikes half past twelve immediately)* I shall see when the clock strikes one! *(The clock suddenly strikes a quarter to one)* Didn't Marley say the ghost would appear at one? *(The clock strikes one)* The hour itself *(Chuckles)* and nothing else!

(A spirit is standing next to Scrooge. It holds a sprig of holly in its hand, and is the size of a child)

Scrooge: *(Turns and sees the figure)* Who… who and what are you?

Christmas Past: I am the Ghost of Christmas Past.

Scrooge: *(Not afraid but curious)* Long past?

22

Christmas Past:	*Your* past. I am here for *your* good. *(Takes Scrooge firmly by the arm)* Come and walk with me.
Scrooge:	*(Notices the ghost is making for the window, which is opening. Afraid)* No, I can't go through the window, this is not the ground floor and I am human. The fall would kill me.
Christmas Past:	*(Gentle)* Just touch my arm, no harm will come to you!
	(The Spirit of Christmas Past and Scrooge fly through the open window. Soon, they are both in the open countryside. They arrive at a village. It is a cold winter's day. The ground is covered with snow)
Scrooge:	*(Amazed)* I was bred in this place. I was a boy here! I remember the odours in the air, they are smells I remember from my childhood.
Christmas Past:	*(Smiling)* You know the place?
Scrooge:	*(Excited)* Know it? I could walk it blindfold!
Christmas Past:	*(Musing)* Strange you forgot it for so many years.
	(Scrooge and Christmas Past walk along the road)
	(Pointing out to Scrooge) There are children in

great spirits, shouting at one another and laughing. Everyone is happy. These are shadows of the things that have been. The children are not aware of us. Look Scrooge, they are coming out of school. But there is one lonely child, forgotten by his friends. He is still in school.

Scrooge: *(Sobs)* I know, I know! It's me!

(The young Scrooge enters and sits. He is reading)

I used to believe the characters I read came to life, came to see me. Ali Baba, Robinson Crusoe, Man Friday… *(Suddenly thinks of his former self)* Poor boy! I wish… but it's too late now!

Christmas Past: What's the matter?

Scrooge: *(Upset)* There were children singing Christmas carols near my door. I should have given them something – that's all!

Christmas Past: *(Waves his hand)* Come on, let's see another Christmas.

(The young Scrooge exits. A taller and older boy, Scrooge, appears. Again, he is alone in the classroom. Soon, the door is opened and a young girl rushes in)

Fan: *(Very excited)* I have come to bring you home, dear brother! Isn't that great news?

Young Scrooge:	*(Surprised)* Home, Fan?
Fan:	Home for good and all. Home forever and ever. Father spoke to me gently one night. He said that you were to come home. He sent me in a coach to bring you home! We'll all be together at Christmas and have the merriest time in all the world.

(Fan and the young Scrooge exit)

Christmas Past:	*(Looks at Scrooge)* Your sister, Fan, always a delicate creature whom a breath might have withered – but she had a large heart.
Scrooge:	*(Upset)* So she had, you are right.
Christmas Past:	She died a young woman… and had, I think, children.
Scrooge:	One child.
Christmas Past:	Your nephew.
Scrooge:	Yes!

(The Ghost of Christmas Past takes Scrooge by the arm and they fly upwards, only landing when they arrive at the city. It is another cold Christmas Eve. The spirit and Scrooge are outside a warehouse door)

26

Christmas Past:	Do you know this place?
Scrooge:	*(Excited)* I was an apprentice here! *(Inside the warehouse, behind a desk, sits a well dressed old man)* Why, it's old Fezziwig! Bless his heart, it's Fezziwig, alive again!
Fezziwig:	*(Calling in a comfortable, rich, happy voice)* Yo ho there! Ebenezer! Dick! *(The young Scrooge, now a young man, walks briskly in, accompanied by Dick Wilkins, another apprentice)*
Scrooge:	*(Happy)* Why, it's Dick Wilkins, to be sure! He was a good friend of mine in those days.
Fezziwig:	*(To his apprentices)* Yo ho, my boys! No more work tonight. It's Christmas Eve, boys. Let's have the shutters up and clear away, my lads. Make space for cold roast beef and cake and mince pies. We'll have a jolly good time before you go to your homes. Christmas comes but once a year, yo ho!
Christmas Past:	A small matter for Mr Fezziwig to make you apprentices happy.

Scrooge: A small matter! I… I wish I could say a word or two to my clerk, Bob, just now.

Christmas Past: We must move on, time is short.

(The young Scrooge, Fezziwig and Dick exit. Then the young Scrooge re-enters with Bella, a pretty young girl who is wearing a mourning dress. Young Scrooge has changed. He is looking mean and his restless eyes suggest greed. They sit on a grassy mound)

Bella: *(Sobs)* Another idol has replaced me. If it can cheer and comfort you in time to come, as I would have tried to do, I have no cause to grieve.

Young Scrooge: *(Sneers)* What idol has replaced you, Bella?

Bella: Gold, money!

Young Scrooge: Poverty is a hard thing. I am trying to become rich for *our* sake, Bella.

Bella: You fear the world too much. The only master – passion – you have is gain. *(Sobs)* It's such a pity, you are basically a good man. Gain and greed are taking over your life.

Young *(Annoyed)* I am not *changed* towards you,

Scrooge: Bella.

(Bella shakes her head)

Am I?

Bella: *(Acts as if in pain)* Our engagement was made a long time ago. It was made when we were both poor and happy to be so. We were to marry when, by hard work, our fortunes would improve. *(Sobs)* You were a different person then.

Young Scrooge: *(Sneers)* I was a boy then!

Bella: *(Upset)* I'm not sure we can be happy together anymore. I release you from our engagement… so you can pursue money and wealth.

Young Scrooge: *(Surprised)* I have not sought release from our engagement.

Bella: Inwardly, no. But your nature is so changed – your spirit is so altered. You do not value my love anymore. You do not *need* me. *(Stands up)* You will forget me, like an unprofitable dream! *(Cries)* May you be happy in the life you have chosen. *(Exits)*

Scrooge: *(Upset)* Spirit, show me no more. Take me home! Why do you enjoy torturing me?

Christmas Past:	(*Firm*) One shadow more.
Scrooge:	(*Covering his eyes*) No more! I don't wish to see it! Show me no more! No more! (*Young Scrooge exits. Older Bella enters. She is now middle-aged. Sits next to a warm fire. Her daughter, who looks exactly like she did, is reading. Walking into the room is an upright man, about Bella's age. His daughter greets him with a kiss. He kisses Bella and sits next to her*)

Husband: *(Warming his hands by the fire)* Bella, guess what? I saw an old friend of yours this very afternoon.

Old Bella: *(Surprised)* Who was it?

Husband: *(Teasing)* Guess!

Old Bella: How can I? Tut, don't I know. *(Laughs)* Mr Scrooge!

Husband: *(Laughs)* Mr Scrooge it was. I passed his office window. He had a small candle inside. I could scarcely help but see him. His partner lies on the point of death, I hear. There he sat, all alone. Quite alone in the world, I do believe.

Scrooge: *(Turns to the spirit)* Remove me from this place!

Christmas Past: I told you these were shadows of the things that have been. They are what they are, do not blame me!

Scrooge: Take me home, take me home. I cannot bear it!

(The ghost swiftly exits. Scrooge finds himself alone in his room. Feeling exhausted, he falls into his chair and sinks into a deep, heavy sleep)

Scene Four

Scrooge is fully awake. He wanders around his room. It is decked with holly, mistletoe and ivy. Christmas food is everywhere, as if somebody is about to hold a banquet. In the middle of all the food sits a jolly giant. He is dressed in a simple green robe, bordered with white fur. On his head, there is a holly wreath. The giant's hair is brown and curly

Christmas Present: *(Beckons Scrooge)* Come near! Come near and know me better!

(Scrooge timidly approaches the giant)

I am the Ghost of Christmas Present, look at me! Have you never seen the like of me before?

Scrooge: *(Shakes his head)* Never. *(Pauses)* Spirit, conduct me where you will. Last night I learned a valuable lesson. Tonight, if you have anything to teach me, let me learn!

Christmas Present: Touch my robe.

(Scrooge is taken above the snow-filled streets. He can see all the happy, cheerful people. Some are throwing snowballs at each other, others are eating chestnuts and others are making their way to church. Scrooge and the spirit fly on, until they

come to Bob Cratchit's house. There they stop –
and see Mrs Cratchit and two of her many
children. They are in the small dining room)

Mrs Cratchit: *(Laughing)* Whatever has got into your precious
father then? And your brother, Tiny Tim. And
Martha warn't as late last Christmas day by half
an hour.

Belinda: Here's Martha, Mother.

Peter: Here's Martha, Mother. Hurrah! There's *such* a
goose, Martha!

Mrs Cratchit: Why, bless your heart alive, my dear, how late
you are!

Martha: We'd a deal of work to finish up last night…
and had to clear away this morning, Mother.

Mrs Cratchit: *(Laughs)* Never mind! So long as you are all
here. Sit down by the fire and have a warm
drink.

Peter: *(Excited)* There's Father coming. *(To Martha)*
Come on, let's hide.

(Bob enters, his threadbare clothes darned up and
brushed to look good for Christmas. Tiny Tim is
on his shoulders. He is holding a crutch and his
tiny limbs are supported by an iron frame)

Bob: *(Puzzled)* Why, where's our Martha?

Mrs Cratchit: *(Trying to look serious)* Not coming.

Bob: *(Disappointed)* Not coming? Not coming on Christmas Day!

(Martha jumps out and runs to greet Bob. Peter and Belinda hug Tiny Tim)

Mrs Cratchit: *(To Bob)* Well, how did Tiny Tim behave?

Bob: *(Smiles)* As good as gold. *(Pauses)* You know how he gets – thoughtful. He sits by himself too much! He thinks the strangest things you've ever heard. He told me, coming home, that he hoped people would see him in church, because he was a cripple, and it might be pleasant for them to remember on Christmas Day, who made the lame beggars walk and blind men see.

Mrs Cratchit: Our poor boy!

Bob: *(Putting on a brave face but not convincing)* Tiny Tim is growing strong and hearty.

Mrs Cratchit: *(Shouts)* Come on everyone, the goose is cooked.

Peter: And I've mashed the potatoes.

(The Cratchit family tuck into their Christmas dinner as it is bought to them by Mrs Cratchit and Belinda. Every scrap of goose is eaten)

Mrs Cratchit: Oh, now for the pudding. *(She dashes out of the room)*

Peter: Hurrah!

Belinda: *(Worried)* Suppose it should not be done enough?

Peter: *(Teasing)* Suppose somebody should have got over the wall of the back yard and stolen it!

Bob: Hello, a great deal of steam.

Mrs Cratchit: *(Returning with the pudding. It is very small for a large family)* Here it is!

(All laugh and shout, no one will spoil the fun by saying that they have to make do with what they can afford)

Tiny Tim: Oh no, the pudding's on fire!

Bob: *(Kindly)* Your mother set the pudding alight with brandy. It's a tradition and it won't spoil the pudding.

Peter: Yum yum!

Bob: *(Claps his hands. There is silence)* A Merry Christmas to us all, God bless us.

Tiny Tim: *(Enthusiastic)* God bless everyone.

Bob: *(Holds Tiny Tim's withered hand)* And may the Lord keep you with us, Tiny Tim.

Mrs Cratchit: *(Shocked)* Bob!

Scrooge: *(To the spirit)* Tell me, will Tiny Tim live?

Christmas Present: I see a vacant seat in the poor chimney corner, and a crutch without an owner, carefully kept. If these shadows remain as they are, unaltered by the future, the child will die!

Scrooge: *(Upset)* No, no. Oh no, kind spirit. Say he will be spared.

Christmas Present: *(Matter of fact)* If these shadows remain, he will not be found here. If he'd rather die, he'd better do it!

(Scrooge, on hearing his own words quoted back to him, hangs his head in shame. He quickly raises his head when he hears his own name mentioned)

Bob: *(Raises his glass)* Mr Scrooge! I'll give you Mr Scrooge, the founder of this feast!

Mrs Cratchit: *(Angry)* Founder of the feast indeed! I wish I had him here…

(Scrooge cringes)

I'd give him a piece of my mind to feast upon and I hope he'd have a good appetite for it!

Bob: (*Puts his glass down*) My dear, the children! Christmas Day!

Mrs Cratchit: (*Bangs the table*) It *should* be Christmas Day, I am sure, on which one drinks the health of such an odious, stingy, hard, unfeeling man as Mr Scrooge.

(*Scrooge winces*)

You know I speak the truth, Robert. Nobody knows it better than you do, you poor fellow!

Bob: (*Mild*) My dear, Christmas Day!

Mrs Cratchit: (*Raises her glass*) I'll drink his health for your sake, my dear Bob and *not* for his. Long life to him! A Merry Christmas and a Happy New Year! (*Sarcastic*) He'll be very merry and very happy, I have no doubt!

Christmas Present: (*To Scrooge*) *You* are the ogre of the family. The mention of your name has cast a dark shadow on the party.

Bob: (*To Peter*) I've found a job for you to do, Peter. It'll bring in some more money – if you get the job.

Martha: (*Yawns*) I'll have a day off tomorrow and I'll lie in bed and have a real rest.

Tiny Tim: *(Begins to sing)* There was a lost child, travelling in the snow.

Christmas Present: *(To Scrooge)* Come on, the snow is falling fast. We must leave this place.

Scrooge: *(Upset)* But Tiny Tim… his song….

(The spirit has a firm grip on Scrooge and they leave the Cratchit home to travel elsewhere. They arrive at Scrooge's nephew's house)

Nephew: *(Kisses his wife. They both laugh)* He told me Christmas was a humbug. He believed it too!

Niece: Shame on him, Fred.

Nephew: *(Suddenly serious)* He's a funny old fellow and that's the truth. Not so pleasant as he might be. However, his offences carry their own punishment and I have nothing to say against the old man.

Niece: I'm sure he is very rich, Fred.

Nephew: What of that, my dear? His wealth is of no use to him. He don't do any good with it. He don't make himself comfortable with it. He hasn't even the satisfaction of thinking *(He laughs)* that he is ever going to benefit *us* with it!

Niece: *(Stamps her foot)* I have *no* patience with the man!

40

Nephew: (*Quietly*) Oh, I have! I am sorry for him. I couldn't be angry with him if I tried. Who suffers by his ill whims? Himself – always. He takes it into his head to dislike us and he won't come and dine with us. What's the consequence? He doesn't get to eat with us! He loses some pleasant moments, which could do him no harm.

Niece: (*Thinking*) So… you go and see him and he gives you the cold shoulder.

Nephew: (*Earnest*) He may grumble at me every Christmas Eve till he dies but I'll still call and be in good temper with him. You see, I pity him. (*Picks up his glass of wine*) Well, a Merry Christmas and a Happy New Year to the old fool. He wouldn't take it from me, but he may have it nevertheless. Uncle Scrooge! (*He downs the wine*)

Christmas Present: (*To Scrooge*) Come on, we must see how others celebrate Christmas!

(*The twosome travel far and wide, seeing everyone happy, whatever their circumstances. Scrooge notices the spirit's hair has turned grey*)

Scrooge: (*Shocked*) You are old, so old!

(*The spirit vanishes and Scrooge feels his own grey hair*)

So old!

Scene Five

(A gloomy looking spirit, draped in a long dark cloak, appears. It is hooded and comes towards Scrooge, holding out its hand and moving like mist along the ground)

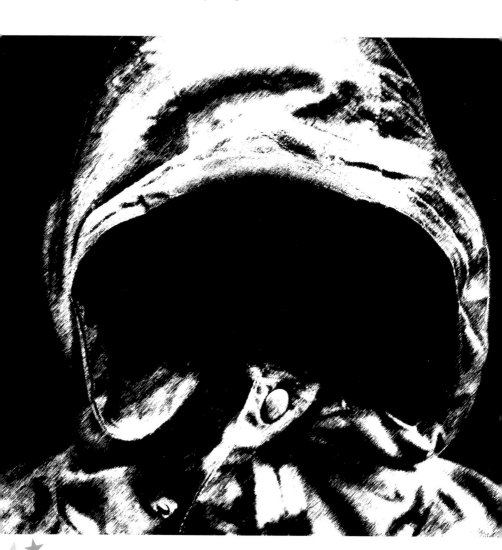

Scrooge: *(Almost cheerful)* Are you the ghost of Christmas yet to come?

(The spirit remains silent but points with its hand)

Are you about to show me the shadows of the things that have not happened, but will happen in the future?

(The spirit gives an almost imperceptible nod)

Ghost of the Future, I fear you more than the other ghosts I've seen. *(Cheerful)* But I know you are here to do me good: therefore I'm prepared to bear your company. Will you speak to me?

(The arm points onwards)

Lead on, lead on, oh Spirit of the Future!

(They arrive at a merchant's house. Some people in the house are talking)

Fat Merchant: I don't know much about it, either way. I only know he's dead.

Thin Merchant: When did he die?

Fat Merchant: *(Shrugs shoulders)* Last night, I believe.

Dark-haired Merchant:	Why, what was the matter with him? I thought he'd never die!

(They all laugh)

Red-faced Merchant:	*(Sneaky)* What's he done with the money, eh?

Fat Merchant:	I haven't heard. *(Shrugs shoulders)* Left it to his company, perhaps? *(Mock confidentially)* He hasn't left it to *me,* that's all I know.

(They all laugh again)

It's likely to be a cheap funeral for I don't know of anyone who'll want to go to it. Suppose we all volunteer?

Red-faced Merchant:	I'll go if a free lunch is provided.

(They laugh yet again)

Fat Merchant:	I don't like wearing funeral clothes and I never eat lunch, but I'll go if you lot do. Come to think of it, I was probably his best mate. We used to stop and speak whenever we met. Well, must be getting along. Bye!

(The merchants go their own ways, still laughing. Scrooge follows the spirit into a dirty, smelly part of the city. A ragged woman is holding a bundle of clothes. She enters a dirty parlour, where Mrs Dilber is standing)

Woman: *(Indicating the bundle)* Who's the worse for the loss of a few things like these? Not a dead man, I suppose!

Mrs Dilber: *(Nods)* No, indeed.

Woman: If he wanted to keep 'em after he was dead, why wasn't he natural in his lifetime? If he had been, he'd have had somebody to look after him when he was struck with death, instead of lying gasping out his last there, alone by himself.

Mrs Dilber: *(Nods)* It's the truest word what was ever spoke. *(Curious)* Anyways, what's in the bundle?

Woman: Oh, his best shirt, his suit, even bed curtains and blankets. I can't let them go to waste when I can sell 'em, can I? He frightened everyone away from him when he was alive, to profit us now he's dead. *(She laughs)*

Scrooge: *(Watches in horror. Turns to the spirit, terrified)* The case of this unhappy man might be my own. My life tends that way now. But who is this man? Does nobody care for him?

(Follows the ghost until they arrive at Bob Cratchit's door)

Ah, the Cratchit household. I see the mother and Belinda. They are knitting. Ah, there's Peter, reading. But why are they so quiet?

Mrs Cratchit: *(Dull voiced)* Father should be home soon!

Peter: *(Sad)* He walks a little slower than he once did.

(They are all quiet for a while)

Mrs Cratchit: *(Tries to be cheerful)* I have known him walk – I have known him walk with Tiny Tim upon his shoulders, very quickly indeed.

Peter: And so have I – often!

Mrs Cratchit: *(Sadly)* But Tiny Tim was so very light to carry and his father loved him so that it was no trouble, no trouble. *(A knocking is heard)* And there is your father, at the door.

Bob: *(Walks in, slowly, as if he is carrying a great weight. Speaks with forced cheerfulness)* Why, my dear wife, the knitting is splendid. Oh, Belinda – what a good job you are doing. Peter, you have chopped the wood for the fire. What a wonderful family I have! *(Pause)* I walked there today, my dear. I wish you could have gone, to see how green the place was. I promised him I would walk there on Sundays, but I had to go today. *(He sits at the table and puts his head in his hands)* My little child, my little, little child.

(Bob weeps, Mrs Cratchit moves over to him. She places a tender hand on his shoulder)

I met a pleasant gentleman today, I met Mr Scrooge's nephew. He wanted to be of service to us, in any way he could. It was as if he knew our Tiny Tim, and felt with us.

Mrs Cratchit: I'm sure he's a good man, so unlike his uncle.

Bob: *(Confident)* I'm sure he's going to find Peter a better job, one that pays more.

Mrs Cratchit: *(Pleased)* Hear that, Peter? We shall all be proud of you!

Peter: *(Embarrassed)* Get along with you!

Bob: *(Thinking)* Peter will set up for himself one day and move out of this house, to start his own. *(Serious)* Not yet, but in the far-distant future. When you children do part from us, when we part from one another, I'm sure none of you will forget poor Tiny Tim, shall you… or this first parting that there was amongst us?

Children: Never, Father!

Bob: And when we realise how kind and patient Tiny Tim was, we shall not easily quarrel amongst ourselves and forget Tiny Tim in doing it.

Children: No, Father. Never, Father!

Bob: *(Smiles)* Then I am very happy.

Scrooge: (*In tears*) Poor Tiny Tim. (*Thinking*) Spectre, I know we must soon part, so tell me, who was that man we know has died?

(*The ghost walks slowly and Scrooge follows him. They arrive at Scrooge's office. Scrooge peers through the window. The furniture has changed and the person sitting at the new desk is not Scrooge. The ghost walks on*)

Where are we going? That's my office. Who is that, sitting there?

(*Scrooge is led into a graveyard*)

Are these future shadows things that *will* be or things that *may* be?

(*The Ghost of Christmas Future points down to a particular grave. Scrooge peers at an overgrown and weed-strewn headstone*)

Surely, men's actions may lead to certain ends. But if men's actions change, surely the ends will change? (*He kneels down by the gravestone and peers at the name. He lets out a long gasp – the name is his own!*) I'm that man the merchants were talking about! I'm that man whose clothes the two women were looking through in the dirty part of the city. I'm the man who died alone, without a friend in the world. Spirit, I

have learned lessons. From now on, I will honour Christmas in my heart. *(He grabs hold of the gloomy spirit)* Oh, save me from this dreadful end.

(The spirit moves away and Scrooge finds himself all alone, in his own room)

Scene Six

Scrooge jumps from his chair

Scrooge: *(To himself)* I will live in the past, the present and the future. I will put everything right! I *will* change the future! *(He laughs)* I am as light as a feather, as happy as an angel, as merry as a schoolboy. I'm as giddy as a drunken man. *(He opens the window and shouts through it)* A Merry Christmas to everybody! A Happy New Year to all the world. *(Scrooge laughs)* How long was I with the spirits? I don't know what day of the month it is. *(In the distance, Scrooge hears the church bells ringing. He spies a boy, dressed in Sunday clothes)* Hey, boy, what day is it? Why are the church bells ringing?

Boy: Eh?

Scrooge: What day is it, my fine fellow?

Boy: *(Puzzled)* Eh? Today? Why, it's Christmas Day!

Scrooge: *(To himself)* It's Christmas Day? I haven't missed it! The spirits have all visited me in one night! They can do anything they like. Of course they can. Of course they can! *(To the boy)* Hallo, my fine fellow!

Boy: *(Indicating with his finger that Scrooge has a screw loose)* Hallo!

50

Scrooge: Do you know the shop in the next street? It sells turkeys, does it not?

Boy: Know it? I should hope I do!

Scrooge: Do you know whether they've sold the prize turkey that was hanging up there? Not the little prize turkey, but the big one.

Boy: *(Still puzzled)* What, the one as big as me? It's hanging there now.

Scrooge: *(Excited)* Is it? Go and buy it.

Boy: *(Raises his eyes to the heavens)* Joker!

Scrooge: *(Grins)* No, no, I mean it. Go and buy it and tell 'em to bring it here, that I might give them directions as to where to take it. Come back with the man and I'll pay you a good tip.

(The boy runs off, eager to make some money)

(To himself) I'll send it to Bob Cratchit's house. He won't know who sent it. It's twice the size of Tiny Tim!

(The man and boy arrive with the turkey. Scrooge pays the boy)

Man: Hallo!

Scrooge: *(Sees the turkey)* What a turkey! Merry Christmas! *(Looks at the turkey)* Why, it's impossible to carry that to Camden Town, you must hire a cab. Lawrence cabs are the best, you must get one! *(Walks out into the street)* Merry Christmas, everyone!

(A number of people wish Scrooge a Merry Christmas)

Scrooge: Good morning everyone, a Merry Christmas to you all!

(The boy indicates to the man that he thinks Scrooge is mad, the man nods in agreement. Scrooge has not gone far when he meets the two gentlemen who had been collecting for charity)

My dear sirs, how do you do? I hope you succeeded collecting all the money yesterday. It was very kind of you both. You gave up some of your valuable time for a good cause. A Merry Christmas, sirs.

Gentleman 1: *(Surprised)* Mr Scrooge?

Scrooge: *(Happy)* Yes, that is my name and I fear it may not be a pleasant one to either of you gentlemen. *(Bows)* Allow me to ask your pardon. And will you have the goodness to allow a donation of...? *(Scrooge whispers the large amount in the gentlemen's ears)*

Gentleman 2: Lord bless me!

Gentleman 1: *(Shocked)* My dear Mr Scrooge, are you serious?

Scrooge: *(Laughs)* If you please... not a penny less. A great many back-payments are included in the amount given, I assure you. Will you do me that favour?

Gentleman 2: *(Staggered)* My dear sir, we are lost for words!

Scrooge: *(Happy to give away vast amounts of money)* Don't say another word. Will you both come and see me from time to time?

Gentleman 1: We will.

Gentleman 2: We *certainly* will!

Scrooge: Thank 'ee both. I am much obliged. Bless you both.

(Scrooge crunches his way through the snow until he reaches his nephew's house. He walks past the

house and back again, until he has the courage to knock on the door. It is opened by a servant girl)

Scrooge: *(Nervous)* Is your master at home, my dear?

Servant: *(Bright)* Yes sir, he is sir.

Scrooge: *(Bolder)* Where is he, my love?

Servant: He's in the dining room, sir, along with the mistress. I'll show you upstairs, if you please.

Scrooge: Thank 'ee. He knows me. I'll introduce myself. *(Walks into the dining room)* Fred!

Nephew: *(Turns, surprised to hear Scrooge's voice)* Why bless my soul, who is that? My uncle?

Scrooge: *(Smiles)* Yes, it's I, your Uncle Scrooge. I have come to dine with you. Will you let me in, Fred?

Nephew: *(Walks over to Scrooge and shakes him by the hand. Happy)* Let you in? Why, you are most welcome. Isn't he, my dearest?

(Fred's wife nods and laughs)

Scrooge: *(Narrating)* I had the best time I'd had for years. I can tell you, I walked home a very happy man!

Scene Seven

Scrooge is early to arrive at his office the following morning. He is dressed in his usual work clothes. Bob is almost eighteen minutes late, which is what Scrooge had hoped would happen

Scrooge: *(Growling)* Hallo! What do you mean by coming in at this time of day?

Bob: *(Subdued)* I am very sorry, sir. I *am* behind time.

Scrooge: *(Gruff)* You are! Yes, I think you are. Step this way, sir, if you please!

Bob: *(Pleading)* It's only once a year, sir! It shall not be repeated, sir. I was making rather merry yesterday, sir.

Scrooge: *(Softer voice)* Now, I'll tell you what, my friend. I am not going to stand this sort of thing any longer. *(Leaps from his chair)* And therefore… I am about to… *raise* your salary!

(Bob is afraid Scrooge has gone mad. He grabs a ruler from the desk, ready to defend himself)

A Merry Christmas, Bob. *(Slaps Bob on the back)* A merrier Christmas, Bob, my good fellow, than I have given you for many a year. I'll double your salary and help your struggling family. We'll discuss how I can help you this very afternoon – after we have eaten at the very best restaurant in London. (*Laughs*) Make up the fires, Bob. We'll keep this place warm. I'll be a second father to Tiny Tim, he'll grow fit and healthy to be sure. (*Freezes*)

Bob: (*Narrating*) I'm not sure if Mr Scrooge saw any ghosts. Perhaps his conscience got the better of him, or maybe he dreamed of all that he'd known in the past. His future was predictable, because everyone hated him. He didn't need Christmas spirits to tell him what he already knew. I'll leave the ghost problem to you all! What I do know is that Mr Scrooge really did change from that day on. And in case you are wondering, Tiny Tim did grow up to be a fine young man. And Scrooge lived on for many years. (*Laughs*) It was always said of him that he knew how to keep a good Christmas. May that be truly said of us all! (*Smiles at audience*) And a Happy Christmas to you all!

(*They exit*)

Exploring the Play

Scene One

Freeze-framing

In small groups, freeze-frame the moment when the two gentlemen are refused money and Scrooge wants to get rid of them as soon as possible. Concentrate on body language and facial expressions.

Thought tunnel

Choose three characters from the play to walk through a thought tunnel. The actors must keep in role. The rest of the group will whisper how they believe each character will think and feel about what has happened so far.

(A thought tunnel is formed by using the class to create two parallel lines which face each other. Each person in one line touches the person, by fingertip, in the opposite line – thus creating a tunnel. The characters walk through the tunnel slowly, and the other pupils speak his or her 'thoughts' aloud.)

Writing

Write a newspaper report about Jacob Marley's life. It can be an obituary. Make up events about his life and how he came to know Ebenezer Scrooge. Mention how Marley came to be mean, money grabbing and rich. You can also mention his death and how Scrooge reacted at the funeral.

Write a play about Marley's life, mentioning all the events you have written into the newspaper report.

Acting

Act out a scene from your play about Marley's life.

Scenes Two and Three

Chat show

Imagine the people in these scenes have travelled through time and landed in the twenty-first century. In groups, imagine you have the opportunity to interview some of the characters on a television chat show. Write down a number of questions that you would like to ask each character. Take it in turns to ask questions in role.

The characters you could invite on the chat show might be: Scrooge, Marley's ghost, the Ghost of Christmas Past, Mr Fezziwig, Bob Cratchit, Mrs Cratchit, Bella and/or Scrooge's nephew, Fred.

Weakest link

If you were stuck with the above characters on a sinking ship, which one do you feel might let you down? Think about all the virtues and weaknesses of the characters.

Might it be Marley's ghost, because he only looked after himself in life? Or Scrooge, because he has always been mean? Or Mr Fezziwig, because he is too kind and generous to be of any use? Perhaps Bob Cratchit because he should have stood up to Scrooge – or Mrs Cratchit because she is all words and no action? Perhaps Bella is the weakest link because she broke off her engagement to Scrooge and cannot be trusted? Surely Fred is too kind and patient to Scrooge and will be of no use on a sinking ship? As a class, vote off the weakest link!

Storyboarding

Choose two or three key events from scenes two or three and create a storyboard, as if you were making a film of 'A Christmas Carol'. Sketch each frame and describe what the audience will hear.

Scenes Four and Five

Good and bad characters

Do you think the characters portrayed in these two scenes are good or bad, or in between?

Look at the headings below and place each character under one of the following headings:

•GOOD　　•BAD　　•MOSTLY GOOD　　•MOSTLY BAD

Creating a television production

In pairs, look again at the characters in these scenes. Decide which film or television actors you would cast for each role. Write down one or two reasons to support your choices. Compare ideas in a class or group discussion.

Virtues

Who do you think shows positive virtues in the play so far? Who shows the least? Tick the chart below.

	Generous	Caring	Friendly	Honest	Bad Tempered
Scrooge					
Bob					
Nephew					
Tiny Tim					
Fat Merchant					
Mrs Dilber					
Mr Fezziwig					
Bella					

Scenes Six and Seven

Main Themes

In pairs, list what you believe are the main themes in the play.

Drama/writing

You are a reporter for 'The Daily Victorian'. You have heard that Scrooge is a changed man. List some of the questions you might want to ask him. In pairs, take it in turns to be Scrooge and the reporter. The reporter should be able to ask Scrooge five or six questions, related to his role in the play.

Write a newspaper report for 'The Daily Victorian' about Scrooge and his changed attitude towards Christmas. You will need to think about:

• A catchy headline, such as 'Mean Old Man Turns Into Santa'.

• How mean Scrooge once was – not giving money to charity, not caring about Marley's death and treating his workforce badly. Include an account of this in your report.

• *Why* Scrooge changed. How he saw four ghosts.

• *How* Scrooge changed. He is now looking after his workforce and his employee's sick boy. He is now very generous at Christmas. He is now kind to people and has many friends.